Story by Mike Wilson
Illustrations by Chris Seiter

For as long as he could remember –
years, maybe –
a hundred years, maybe –
well, say five years, anyway –
Dexter had lived in the castle.
Life was not easy for the littlest knight
in the castle.
The King's Champion, the Green Knight,
was in charge of all the other Knights,
and he kept Dexter working
all the time.

Dexter was always the one who had to blow the dragon's nose when it had a cold.

Dexter was always the one who had to drain the moat for spring cleaning.

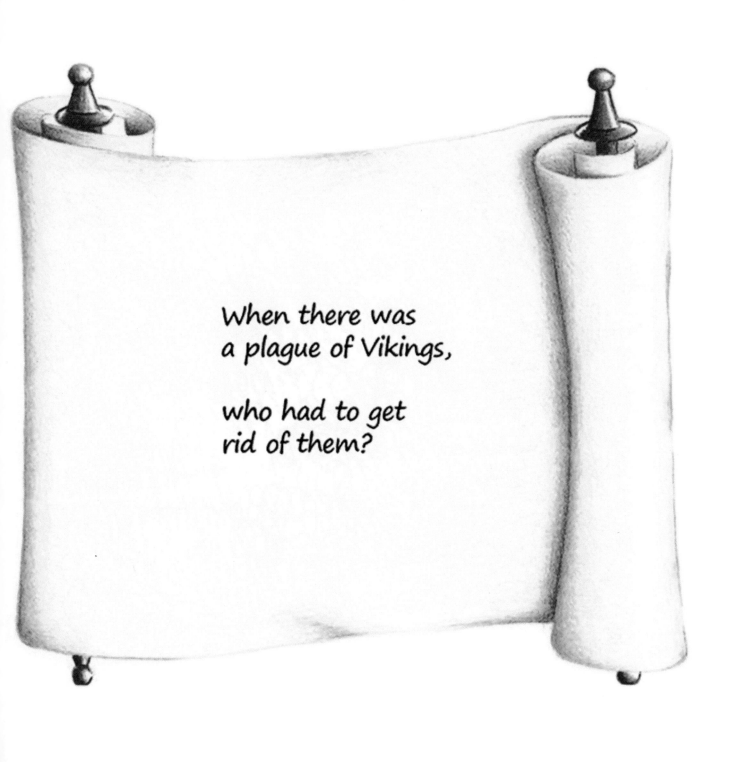

When there was
a plague of Vikings,

who had to get
rid of them?

Dexter.

When it began
raining Wizards,

who had to
catch them?

When the old tower burned down,
fell over, and
sank into the mud,

who had to build a new one?

Dexter.

What Dexter really wanted to do
was compete in the
jousting tournament!

But every year, he had been
too little to ride.

This year he was
sure he was big enough!

He put on his armor
and went to see the King.

But the King said "No" again.

Dexter was sad,
so he went to see his friend William,
the King's Weasel Counselor.

Most kings kept a Weasel around,
to give them advice. Some had several.
A lot of kings had natural Weasel abilities,
and didn't need an actual Weasel.

One of Dexter's jobs was to change
the papers for William.

William was
hard at work.

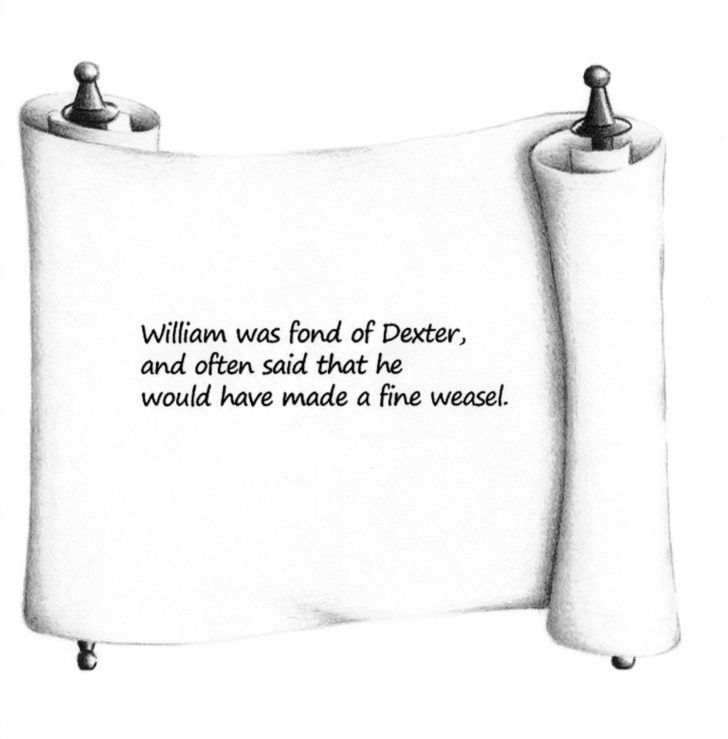

William was fond of Dexter, and often said that he would have made a fine weasel.

Dexter told William about his problem.
William liked problems,
and he liked to invent contraptions
to solve them.
He took Dexter into
his problem-solving room.

It didn't take William long to come up with a contraption to solve Dexter's problem.

On the day of the tournament,
Dexter got ready to joust.

He shined his armor,
decorated his lance,
put on his new jousting shoes,
and climbed onto William's
new contraption.

He would joust under a new name,
to honor his friend:
Weaslodex the Magnificent!

There was only one knight left to defeat, and Dexter would be the king's champion for the year!

The Green Knight.
The King's Champion for the last four years.

The meanest, toughest, greenest knight of them all.

They called him the Green Knight because all the other knights turned green at the thought of jousting him.

Well, that, and because he wore green armor.

Dexter had never been more scared.

Not on Take-A-Zombie to Lunch Day.

Not during the tiny witch convention that filled the castle with tiny flying broomsticks at eye level.

Not even during the castle's annual flu shots.

As scared as he was, though, Dexter and William had a plan.

The Green Knight lined up at one end of the jousting field.

Weaslodex the Magnificent lined up at the other.

The sun shone. Birds sang. Dogs barked.

Minstrels helped themselves to the buffet table.

The smell of flowers drifted through the air.

The King sneezed.

He was allergic to flowers.

With that sneeze, the Green Knight
and his horse charged toward Dexter!

Weaslodex the Magnificent
charged toward the Green Knight!

And – as the Green Knight was almost
upon him – Dexter pushed a button
on Weaslodex the Magnificent,
which released a hatch underneath
Weaslodex the Magnificent, and . . .

. . . released the marbles!
Big marbles, little marbles,
Blue, pink, orange, purple,
yellow, and green marbles.

14,136 marbles,
to be precise.

The Green Knight slid past Dexter.
Dexter ducked desperately, dodging deftly.
The Green Knight crashed to the ground.

When the last marble had stopped rolling,
and everything was quiet again,
Weaslodex the Magnificent was
the new King's Champion!

The mighty Weaslodex stood before
the King.

The King beamed happily at his
new champion.

And that was when Dexter popped the hatch on his armor, and he and William climbed out of Weaslodex.

The King was furious. "No mechanical contraption is going to be my Champion!" he bellowed.

"Don't you want your Champion to be clever?" William asked the King.

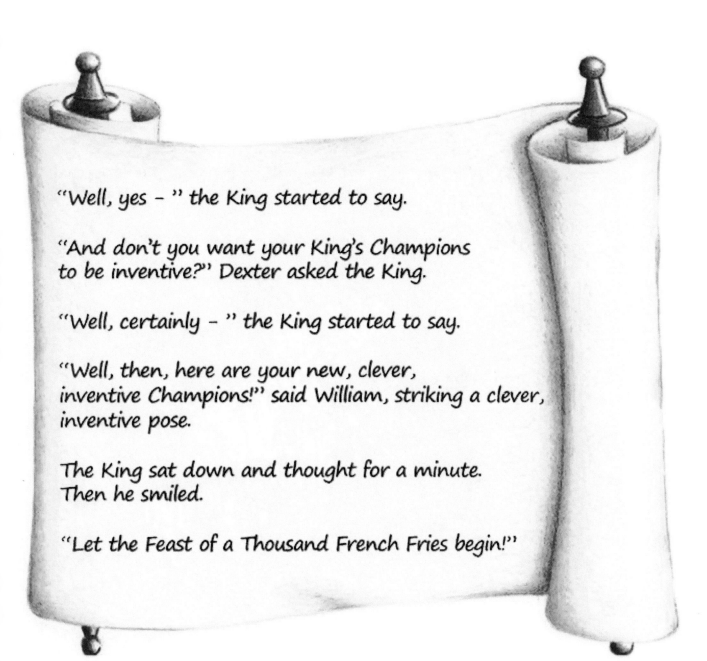

"Well, yes – " the King started to say.

"And don't you want your King's Champions to be inventive?" Dexter asked the King.

"Well, certainly – " the King started to say.

"Well, then, here are your new, clever, inventive Champions!" said William, striking a clever, inventive pose.

The King sat down and thought for a minute. Then he smiled.

"Let the Feast of a Thousand French Fries begin!"

It turned out that as good as William was at inventing contraptions, he was even better at eating French Fries.

It was something about the snout.

There was only one thing
that worried Dexter.

What was a King's Champion
supposed to do?

It was going
to be an
interesting
year.

Visit www.littlestknight.com
for free coloring pages!

Dexter and William will be back in

The Littlest Knight

and

The Giant Problem

Printed in Great Britain
by Amazon

27458516R00023